Spoiled Rotten

Dayle Campbell Gaetz

Orca currents

ORCA BOOK PUBLISHERS

National Library of Canada Cataloguing in Publication Data

Gaetz, Dayle, 1947-
Spoiled rotten / Dayle Campbell Gaetz.

(Orca currents)
ISBN 1-55143-474-1

I. Title. II. Series.

PS8563.A25317S68 2005   jC813'.54   C2005-904075-0

Summary: Jessica must trek through bear country to save her stepsister.

First published in the United States, 2005
Library of Congress Control Number: 2005929721

Orca Book Publishers gratefully acknowledges the support for its publishing
programs provided by the following agencies: the Government of Canada
through the Book Publishing Industry Development Program (BPIDP), the
Canada Council for the Arts, and the British Columbia Arts Council.

Cover design: Lynn O'Rourke
Cover photography: First Light

Orca Book Publishers   Orca Book Publishers
PO Box 5626, Stn. B   PO Box 468
Victoria, BC Canada   Custer, WA USA
V8R 6S4   98240-0468

www.orcabook.com
Printed and bound in Canada
Printed on 50% post-consumer recycled paper,
processed chlorine free using vegetable, low VOC inks.
08 07 06 05 • 4 3 2 1

For Liz,
an all round 'good' person.

chapter one

My hiking boots slopped through soft mud. Cedar branches slapped my face and young alder trees brushed against my knees. The trail was so overgrown it looked like no one had used it since the last time we'd been there.

That was three years ago, before Mom got sick.

Dad veered off the trail in front of me. He pushed through thick undergrowth toward a rocky cliff. This was Mom's favorite place in the whole world. It made me feel good just to be here again. At the same time, something inside me felt like crying.

We climbed up the rocks on all fours. It wasn't a difficult climb, not so steep we needed ropes, but we had to work. At the top Dad and I stood on a moss-covered rock and looked down. The steep, forested hillside dropped away to a sea as blue as the sky. Dark green islands dotted the calm water. In the distance, the white cone of Mount Baker seemed to hang suspended over low hills.

"The top of the world," I whispered.

That's what Mom had always called this place.

Dad nodded. He had been so quiet all morning I knew he had something important to tell me. That's the way he is. Sometimes he takes forever to get words out of his mouth.

We settled on the rocks and unpacked our lunch. I gobbled down two sandwiches and bit into an apple. Dad took one bite of his sandwich and stared at the view.

It was time to help him out. "Did you decide not to marry Patti after all?" I crossed my fingers, hoping he would say yes. Maybe that's why he wanted to come back here, to Mom's place, today.

He looked surprised. "Of course not. Why would I change my mind?"

I glanced around, at the trees, the mountain, our hiking boots. "Oh, I don't know, maybe because she's not your type?"

"Jessica, I love Patti, that's not going to change."

Ouch, that hurt. "But you did tell her we don't want to spend our vacation on her stupid boat?"

"Jess, look, I'm sorry but..."

"I don't believe this! You *want* to go, don't you? What about our hiking trip?" Tears stung my eyes as I turned away. *How could he do this to me?*

"I thought it would be fun to try something different for a change. We can go hiking another time."

So this was his big news? The hiking trip we had planned all year was not going to happen? Too angry to sit still, I leapt up and tossed my apple at him. It bounced off his chest. "I'm not going with you!" I shouted.

Dad stood up too, his face red with anger. "Now you listen to me, Jessica! I'm your father and I say you're coming. Like it or not."

"How could I possibly *like* it?" I asked coolly. It's funny how that worked. The angrier my father got the calmer I felt inside. And the more determined.

He looked at me and daggers shot from his eyes. It hurt almost like real daggers, but I pretended not to care. He threw his arms in the air and took a step toward me. "I don't understand," he said. "We had such a good time last year." He paused and his eyes searched my face. The daggers were replaced with a pleading that twisted at my heart. "Didn't we?" he asked softly.

I leaned my head back and peered down my nose at him. The hard angry line of his jaw softened and his mouth hung open. Dad didn't look so scary now. He looked sad. I knew I could hurt him then, all I had to do was say no.

I stared over his shoulder, away from his face. If I thought about last summer I would turn into mush. We were so close then. My dad had treated me like an equal, even though I had been only thirteen. And he never expected less of me because I was a girl. That was important to me.

"Didn't you enjoy our trip last summer?" he asked weakly.

"Yeah." I had to admit, "It was fun."

I shut the memories behind a black wall in my mind. I couldn't afford to think about the good times because that would make me weak.

"Then what's so different about this year?"

I couldn't believe he would ask such a stupid question.

"Everything!" I shouted. I didn't mean to shout, but there was something about his face that made anger well up inside me.

"Last year..." I paused and lowered my voice. "Last year there was just you and me, a beat-up canoe and two backpacks."

I turned my back and stared down at the treetops. I could not let him see my watery eyes. "This year there's you, me, your precious Patti and her snotty little daughter." I shuddered just thinking about Amy. It was hard to believe she was almost twelve. Amy was worse than the worst nerd in my entire school. She had "perfect little angel" written all over her. In short, she was disgusting.

"Worse than that, we'll all be jammed together on their stupid boat."

I could tell my dad was getting angry again. And that was good. I knew how to deal with his anger. It was the deep, hurting sadness I couldn't handle.

He put his hands on my shoulders and twirled me around to face him. He waved a finger in front of my eyes, so close I blinked. "Don't you ever speak that way about your stepmother and stepsister again."

"They aren't my step-anything."

"They will be by next week. And you're going to have to get used to that."

I glared at him. "Isn't it bad enough that

you caved in to what Patti wants? How could you tell me here, *in Mom's place?*"

His face went pale; he stepped back.

I picked up my pack and started toward the cliff.

"Jessica!" he called. "Wait for me. Don't be so stupid!"

I wasn't stupid, no matter what he said. I stopped to put my backpack on properly and turned around to climb down the rock face.

My father needed to gather up our stuff, so he was a few minutes behind. When I reached the bottom, I didn't wait. I started for the trail. I needed to get away from him.

I pushed through bushes that came up to my waist. My father's words rang in my head: *You're going to have to get used to that.* But I didn't want to.

I didn't want things to change. Until today I had been sure my father would come to his senses. I thought he would realize how wrong Patti was for him. I never thought he would cancel our trip together.

I reached the trail and started down. Anger made me walk fast.

If Dad couldn't see it, why didn't Patti? Why did she want to marry him anyway? They had nothing in common. He liked to paddle a canoe on a quiet lake. She liked a big noisy boat with a smelly engine that polluted the ocean.

Her first husband had been a professor at the University of Victoria. A brainy guy, big time educated. Nice man, until he ran off with a younger woman. Patti hadn't seen him in a year.

Patti was an accountant—a neat clean office-type. So why would she marry a hardworking mechanic who comes home with grease under his fingernails? More to the point: *How could she do this to me?* Didn't she know I would always love my mother? Didn't she realize Dad still loved Mom too? That would never change. There was no room in our lives for Patti, and sooner or later my dad was going to figure it out.

I really hoped it would be sooner.

chapter two

As his wedding day got closer and closer I watched my father, hoping he would come to his senses. I knew the marriage would be a disaster, so how come he couldn't figure it out?

I tried to help him along by acting super grumpy. But he didn't notice. So I stopped talking to him. He didn't notice that either. Then I got to thinking that he might *like* it when I didn't talk, so I started talking all the time, yakking about anything I could think of.

Nothing worked. He walked around the house with a stupid grin on his face like he'd won the lottery or something. It was disgusting.

The wedding day arrived, sunny and warm. It should have been raining. They got married in the chapel at the Victoria hospital where Patti used to work. After her husband ran away, Patti had needed a change so she moved to Salt Spring Island to take a job in our hospital. If only her car hadn't broken down. If only Dad hadn't fixed it for her. If only Mom were here.

Sara didn't want to come to the wedding, but I talked her into it. We dressed in our favorite outfits, long cotton skirts and peasant blouses with beaded bracelets. Long earrings dangled from our ears. We made the jewelry ourselves from beads and seashells and feathers. We looked great.

I wanted to sit at the back of the chapel, but they made us sit at the front with the groom's family. That consisted of Sara and me. And you couldn't really call Sara family, even though she was my best friend. I felt like we were on stage with everyone watching us.

The bride's side was bursting with family—a horde of them in fancy dresses and suits. They sparkled with gold and diamonds.

I stared at the back of my dad's head and concentrated on sending him a message: *Hey, Dad! It isn't too late; you can still get out of it!*

"Do you take this woman to be your lawfully wedded wife?" the minister asked.

I held my breath. *Last chance, Dad. Just say no.*

I waited, closed my eyes. *Please!*

"I do," he said, loud and clear.

At the reception Sara and I stood beside a table loaded with tiny sandwiches cut into triangles, stacks of cheese, grapes, pickles, crackers, dips and fancy little cakes.

"Mmm, this is so good!" Sara said, stuffing her face. "Why don't you try some?" She licked chocolate from her fingers.

"I'm not hungry," I told her. "How could anyone eat at a time like this?"

"Do you really hate her that much?" Sara picked up a turkey sandwich.

"Who? Patti?" I shook my head. "I don't hate her, not exactly. I mean I kind of feel sorry for her in a way. First her husband leaves her, which is bad enough, but look what he left behind."

We both looked over at Amy. She sat with her grandmother and was wearing a tacky pink dress with a matching ribbon stuck in her long, blonde hair. Amy saw me, and a little smile crept over her face. I rolled my eyes and turned away.

"Can you imagine living in the same house with her?"

Sara groaned. "But at least there's only one of her. Try living with my sister and brothers and see how long you survive."

Dad and Patti came over. He looked me up and down and shook his head like he was embarrassed. "My daughter, the born-again hippie," he said.

Patti was all gushy and smiley in her pale

blue suit. Her blonde hair was tucked into a blue hat that looked like an upside down cookie tin. She laughed. "I think they look nice," she said and kissed me on the cheek.

Yuck. I hadn't seen that coming.

"I can hardly wait for our boat trip this summer," she said. "I know we'll get to be such good friends."

I looked up at my dad. But he was watching Patti with that stupid grin on his face. Some lottery.

After the wedding I had exactly one week left to enjoy my life. I stayed at Sara's place while Dad and his charming bride went off on their honeymoon. Now there's something I never want to think about.

"If you don't hate Patti, how come you're so depressed?" Sara asked me one evening. We were sitting in her room with the door locked so her little brother and sister couldn't get in to bug us. As usual, the baby was screaming. Their house was so tiny it was hard to get away from all the noise those little kids made.

"I don't know," I tried to explain. "See, Patti was okay as a friend. After Dad met her she sometimes went for walks with me and we'd talk about..." I paused and took a deep breath. "You know, about things."

"Like what?"

"You know. Things my dad would never understand."

Sara nodded.

By the end of that week I was actually looking forward to Dad and Patti getting home. I figured one stuck-up eleven-year-old had to be better than Sara's madhouse.

Man, was I wrong!

The first thing Amy did was try to take over my room.

"Why should she have the biggest room just because she was here first?" Amy whined. She stood in the hall with a stack of blankets in her arms and a huge scowl on her face.

Her mother was bent over a box of dishes in the kitchen. "Whine all you like," she said. "But I won't let you kick Jessica out of her bedroom. It wouldn't be right."

"Oh, fine!" Amy tossed the blankets on the floor. "So I get stuck with a room the size of a closet! How am I supposed to move around in there with all my stuff?"

"I don't know, Amy," her mother said. "If you can't manage we could give your desk to Jessica. I'm sure she could use it for her artwork."

Amy's jaw dropped. "I'll manage." She picked up the blankets and stomped off to her room.

There were only two weeks left until the big summer vacation, and Dad still hadn't told his dear wife that I wasn't going. It seemed to have slipped his mind. He kept talking about how much fun we were *all* going to have.

I didn't want to admit it, but I was beginning to weaken. I couldn't find any place to stay—one week at Sara's place had cured me of ever wanting to stay there again. And Dad would never let me stay home alone.

Then there was the problem of Amy. If Amy had three weeks to brainwash Dad and Patti, who knew what she might accomplish?

They could come home thinking she was the best daughter in the entire world. And I was just the opposite.

I refused to go down without a fight. That night at dinner I took a deep breath and jumped in. "Did Dad tell you I'm not going on the boat trip?"

Everyone stopped eating and stared at me.

"What do you mean?" Patti asked. "I thought you were looking forward to it."

I shook my head, "I don't like boats."

"But, your dad told me what a wonderful time you had last year on your canoe trip."

I gave her *the look*. Eyes hard, jaw clenched, I rolled my eyes up toward the ceiling. "Key word," I said, "canoe. You paddle a canoe and you sleep under the stars. You are not cooped up in a big boat with a noisy stinky engine that pollutes the water everywhere you go."

Patti looked crushed. She put her fork down. "Well, I don't know what to say. You know, I thought about selling the boat this summer; it was my husband who really liked boating anyway. But then your dad told me how much you would enjoy going up to Desolation Sound."

I turned *the look* on my father.

"I thought it would be good for us," he said, "as a family."

"If we sell *Fanta-sea*," Patti suggested, "we could use the money to take a trip we all planned together."

"*Fanta-sea?*" I said. "That's the boat's name? You've got to be kidding." My voice was lost in Amy's wail.

"No-oo. You can't sell *Fanta-sea* just because of her!" Amy had a whole different *look* from mine. Her bottom lip quivered, and big fat tears rolled down her face.

My father's eyes shot daggers again. "How can you be so selfish, Jessica? The three of us are all excited about going cruising to one of the most beautiful places in the world. And you want to ruin it for everyone."

I looked from his anger, to Patti's hurt, to Amy's tears and knew I was beat. But I didn't need to be happy about it. "Crap!" I shouted and pushed my chair back.

"Watch your language," Dad said.

I stood up. "If I go, you can't make me enjoy it!"

I turned and stomped out of the room.

Tears, one. *The look*, zero.

chapter three

Steering a boat is not like driving a car. In a car you pull over, hit the brakes and stop. Simple. Boats don't have brakes. You need to take the current and the wind into account when you pull up to a dock. So, I had to hand it to Patti: She did a good job of steering the boat up to the gas dock at Powell River.

It was our third day out, and Dad sat beside her on the command bridge, watching, so he could learn what to do. I stood on deck, clutching the bow rope, ready to jump. Amy had disappeared. She was probably reading. Amy was always reading.

We were about two meters from the dock, coming in dead slow. Patti shifted the engine to neutral and let the boat drift in. I watched the gap narrow. My bare toes curled over the wood trim. I waited for the right moment.

"JUMP!"

Dad's shout caught me off guard and I started to fall forward. Dark water stared up at me in the narrow gap between boat and dock. It was either jump or fall in, so I pushed off with my toes and leapt through the air.

I landed heavily on the rough wood of the dock. Somehow I tripped over the rope in my hand and fell sideways. But I never let go of that rope. I scrambled to my feet and eased the boat against the dock.

Dad stepped off to tie the stern rope while I tied the bow. I waited for him to say, "Nice work," or "Well done," or maybe, "Sorry I yelled at you," but he didn't even look my way. He patted the pockets of his shorts. "Anyone seen my wallet?" he asked.

Amy appeared from nowhere. "I'll get it, Dad," she said and disappeared into the cabin.

I stared after her. *Dad*? Since when was he her *dad*? This kid wanted everything that was mine.

Amy jumped onto the dock with the wallet in her hand and a self-satisfied smirk on her face. She glanced at me slyly.

"Thanks Amy," my father said.

I turned away.

While Amy and her mother went to buy groceries, Dad and I filled up the gas and water tanks. I kept thinking about the way Amy called him Dad. It burned me up.

If they thought I would ever call Patti Mom, they had better think again. Patti would never replace my mom. My mother died when I was eleven. I still missed her so much that sometimes, when no one was around, I cried.

Mom had long, shiny black hair, soft brown eyes and a gentle smile. She loved the outdoors. We used to hike in the rain forest and paddle our canoe in the sea. She taught me about the birds and animals of the West Coast. She told me stories about my Native grandmother. Mom was so proud that I looked like my grandmother.

No one would ever believe I belonged in this family. Patti and Amy were both blue-eyed, blonde, and—I hated to admit it—pretty. My father had blue eyes and light brown hair. The three of them looked like they belonged together. I was the odd person out.

I thought about that as I sat on the dock at Powell River and watched Patti and Amy walk back from the store, their blonde hair shining in the sun. Amy wore bright pink shorts and a white T-shirt. She had a stupid pink scrunchy on top of her head to hold her hair back from her face. I hate pink. I figured that's why all of Amy's new clothes were pink.

My father was coiling up the water hose. His blue eyes flashed with anger.

"Why don't you get up and help your mother?" he demanded.

"My mother's dead," I snapped. Suddenly my throat hurt and my eyes burned. I waited for him to start yelling, but he only looked back at me with something like pain in his eyes.

I ran to help with the groceries.

Sun sparkled across rippled water. There wasn't a cloud in sight. I sat on the bow and leaned against the cabin window to sketch a bald eagle. Broad wings outstretched, it glided effortlessly above the tall cedars that grew right down to the water's edge.

Sara would love it here! We could sketch together, hike into the hills, go snorkelling, whatever.

I turned to a fresh sheet in my sketchbook and wrote:

Dear Sara,

If only you could be here instead of The Spoiled Brat, we'd have a great time. You can't imagine what she's like...

"Look at that, Jessica!" my father called.

We rounded a narrow point of land and entered a different world. Ahead, outlined against a bright blue sky, was a chain of jagged mountains bluer than the sea. Their highest peaks were blanketed in snow. The mountains rose straight out of the sea to fifteen hundred meters above our heads. I felt like a tiny speck, a chunk of driftwood floating on the ocean.

We cruised through a channel with forested islands on both sides and those soaring mountains dead ahead until we came to a narrow inlet. We headed up the inlet. On either side of us sheer rock faces rose up to craggy peaks. Little streams and waterfalls gushed down the rocks, disappeared in forests and splashed out into the sea.

We had traveled up the inlet for over an hour when we spotted a small bay and a rocky beach. It looked like the perfect place to stay for a few days to relax, swim and explore.

I stood on the bow as we inched toward shore. That's when I spotted the river. Behind the beach, almost hidden by trees, white water tumbled toward the sea. A zigzag path of light green alder trees through the darker green rain forest marked the river's course down the mountainside. High above everything a mountain peak loomed, white with snow.

I could hardly wait to explore the river. Dad would come with me; he had to. How could he resist?

chapter four

We dropped anchor in the bay. When Patti shut the engine off everything went quiet. The only sound was the murmur of river water rushing over rocks.

"The bottom is rocky here," Patti said, "and it's so deep the anchor rope goes straight down. To be safe, we'll need to tie a stern rope to shore."

"I'll go," I offered.

"Amy will go with you," Dad said.

"Aw...," we both said at once.

"Amy can hold the dinghy while you tie the rope," Dad said firmly.

I didn't bother to answer; I knew when I was beat. So I climbed over the stern onto the swim grid and pulled the dinghy close.

Amy sat in the dinghy's stern with a book on her lap. I rowed while Amy held one end of the rope, and Dad fed the line out from a coil on *Fanta-sea*. A brisk wind made the water choppy and a strong current pushed us sideways. I had to row hard to make headway.

"Hurry up!" my father yelled.

"I'm rowing as fast as I can!" I yelled back.

"The wind is pushing us sideways. If you don't hurry, we'll be on the rocks!" he shouted.

I ignored him.

When the bow bumped against the rocky shore, Amy handed me the rope. I climbed out, leaving her to hold the dinghy. On top of a low bank was a big fir tree with a root that curled out of the ground. I climbed up. The root was strong and solid so I tied the rope around it.

"Okay!" I called.

Dad pulled on the rope until it was tight and *Fanta-sea's* stern swung toward me. Then he disappeared inside the boat. I knew he and Patti were making sandwiches and I could hardly wait to eat. I was starved.

I climbed back down to the beach and saw Amy sitting on a big rock, her nose in her book. Behind her the dinghy bounced over bright waves, drifting away with the current.

"Hey, Amy!" I called.

She looked up slowly and smiled that funny little smile of hers. "This is the best book!" she said. "Want to borrow it when I'm done?"

"You didn't tie up the dinghy!" I yelled.

Her face crumpled. "I thought you did."

"That's what you came for!" I shouted. "You had one simple thing to do. Couldn't you at least hold onto the rope?"

"I guess I forgot," she said and turned to look at the dinghy.

Furious, I ran and snatched the book from her hands. "You better start swimming!"

"Give me my book!" She grabbed for it.

"Not until you bring the dinghy back." I held it over my head, out of her reach.

Amy jumped up and down like a flea, but she couldn't get it. So she stood very still, did the lip quiver thing and whined, "I can't swim!"

I knew she was lying. I mean, give me a break! This kid was almost twelve and spent her summers on a boat.

The dinghy drifted quickly along the shoreline. Someone had to go after it right away or it would reach the river mouth and be pushed out of the bay.

"Don't waste your phoney tears on me, Amy, you're just a spoiled little brat!" I tossed her book onto the beach. It bounced against a rock and splashed into the water.

"I hate you, Jessica!" she screamed, and ran to save her book.

I took off. I ran as fast as I could over loose rocks. When I was even with the dinghy, I plunged into the water. It was surprisingly warm.

I swam with strong strokes and gained quickly on the dinghy. But suddenly the water turned icy around me. I had reached the river mouth where glacial waters spilled into the sea. In front of me the dinghy made a slow half-turn and headed straight out from shore.

The cold water took my breath away. But the dinghy was so close! I put my head down and swam as fast as I could. When I looked again the side of the dinghy was just above my head. I reached for it.

A wave splashed against the dinghy and back into my face. I choked on a mouthful of salt water. Another wave splashed over me. I couldn't breathe, and now the boat was out of reach.

If I could get into the dinghy I would be all right. But it was drifting faster now, caught in the river current. Then I noticed its long yellow rope trailing in the water.

Coughing and sputtering, I fought my way to the rope. My fingers touched it, but it slipped away. I tried again and caught the loop at the very end. I pulled myself along the rope, grabbed the dinghy and climbed over the stern.

I reached for the oars and headed for *Fanta-sea*. But the current and wind pushed against me. I started to shiver in my wet clothes. The cool wind didn't help. Even the hard work of rowing didn't warm me.

I wasn't thinking about Amy when I reached *Fanta-sea* and tied up the dinghy. I was so cold all I could think of was getting inside and into some dry clothes.

Water poured down my legs as I squished across the back deck and looked into the cabin. Dad and Patti were eating sandwiches, drinking iced tea and talking. I could have drowned and they wouldn't have noticed.

"Dad," I said crossly. "Can you pass me a towel?"

His head jerked around. He saw me standing in the doorway, dripping wet. His face went hard. "What the...?"

Patti jumped up and grabbed a beach towel to wrap around my shoulders.

"Did you fall in?" she asked.

"No." I told them what had happened. Everything.

My father took an angry breath. "And here we thought you two would learn to be friends if you spent some time together. But you didn't even try, did you?"

I couldn't believe this! After all the trouble Amy caused, he wanted to blame me?

"It wasn't my fault!"

"You're more than two years older. You should be watching out for her."

"Amy isn't a baby, she just acts like one. She can take care of herself."

We all turned toward the loud voice wailing on shore. "Mom!" Amy called. "Jessica left me here!" She paused. "And I'm hungry!"

Patti looked at me, then at her own daughter.

"So swim out," she called. "I didn't pay for all those swimming lessons for nothing."

chapter five

Amy was too stubborn to swim. She stood on the beach trying to turn the pages of her soggy book. Then she waved it in the air and shouted, "You ruined my book, Jessica!"

I shook my head. This kid was unbelievable. She acted more like a five-year-old than someone who would turn twelve in a week. But I was glad I had told Dad and Patti about the book.

"I'll go get her," Dad offered.

"No." Patti put a hand on his arm. "Her father always gave into her tantrums. It's time she started to grow up."

Patti went back into the cabin where she could keep an eye on Amy without being seen. "Let her sulk for a while. She'll swim out when she thinks we've forgotten about her."

I wrapped the beach towel more tightly around myself, but I couldn't stop my teeth from chattering. So I grabbed some dry clothes and squeezed into the tiny bathroom to get changed. It was the only place on the whole boat where I could get any privacy.

As I dressed I thought about Patti. I knew she was trying to be fair, but that only made it harder to hate her. I didn't need her in my life, and I sure didn't need her spoiled rotten daughter.

I dressed in shorts and a T-shirt. Then I pulled a pair of sweat pants and a sweatshirt over top. I sat at the table and ate a sandwich, but I couldn't face the thought of iced tea. It was too cold.

"Why don't you get into your sleeping bag?" Patti suggested. "I'll bring you some hot chocolate."

I wanted to say no. I wanted to tell her to leave me alone. But the thought of hot chocolate was hard to resist. "Okay," I said through chattering teeth.

Dad glared at me. "Is that any way to answer your mother?"

"She's not..." I stopped. What was the use? We all knew she wasn't my mother but they wanted to pretend she was. By then I was too cold to care. "Thank you, Patti," I said and crawled into my sleeping bag.

Dad brought the hot chocolate to me. I sat up and reached for it. He touched my hand. "You're freezing!" he said.

I wrapped both hands around the hot mug and Dad tucked the sleeping bag up around my ears.

"I'll be back in a minute," he said.

When he returned he gave me a hot-water bottle. "Tuck this against your stomach," he said. "I'm heating up some water for the other bottle."

I hugged the hot-water bottle like a little kid with a teddy bear. I must have had hypothermia. In ice-cold water it only takes a few minutes to lower the body's temperature. When that happens your body can't warm itself up again without help.

Dad brought the second hot-water bottle and slid it against my back. By the time I finished my drink I was beginning to warm up. But I felt really sleepy. I closed my eyes.

I woke up later, so hot I felt sick. The air was stifling and I was stuffed in a sleeping bag with two hot-water bottles. My T-shirt stuck to my back. I moaned and struggled to get out of the sleeping bag.

"Shut up!" Amy said from the bunk above mine. "I'm trying to read."

I opened my eyes and reached for my watch hanging on a hook above my bunk. I looked at it, sat up quickly, and looked again. I couldn't believe it was almost five o'clock. I wriggled out of my sleeping bag.

At eye level, Amy glared at me. "Why aren't you outside?" I asked.

"Because I got a sunburn when you made me stay on the beach."

I talked down to her as if she were three years old. "Amy, I didn't make you stay there. You're the one who forgot how to swim."

"Don't act like you're my mother," she growled.

That night I went to bed when everyone else did. But I couldn't sleep. So I got up in the middle of the night and tiptoed out of the cabin. I crossed the back deck and sat on the stern. The sharp outline of the mountain stood tall and dark above me. Moonlight lit up a patch of snow on the very top.

Gentle waves lapped against the boat and river sounds echoed from rocky crags. Somewhere up on the mountain an owl hooted. It reminded me of other years.

Before Mom got sick all three of us used to go hiking into the mountains together. For the past two summers it had been just the two of us. The summer before, Dad and I paddled up the coast and hiked into the hills. We always liked exploring streams and rivers to find little mountain lakes where no one else went.

This river was a perfect one to follow. With so much water there had to be a lake up there somewhere. If not, it wouldn't really matter. Exploring was the part I liked best.

Dad and I had our backpacks and tents on the boat. Tomorrow I would ask him if we could take off to go hiking together. He owed me that much. I mean, didn't I peacefully accept this trip? Hadn't I been helpful and uncomplaining? I'd used *the look* only when absolutely necessary and had not yet tossed Amy overboard.

chapter six

The next morning I found Dad sitting on a folding chair on the back deck. I watched his eyes follow the winding path of the river and saw the old glimmer of excitement on his face.

"I bet you're right," he said, sipping his coffee. "I bet there's a lake up there."

Patti came out then, carrying a coffee mug. Amy trailed behind her.

"Did I hear something about a lake?" Patti asked.

Oh-oh.

Dad nodded. "Jessica and I might go exploring."

"What about me?" Amy whined.

"This is just between me and my father," I told her. I looked to Dad to confirm it. What I saw did not make me feel good. He looked from Amy to me to Patti with a lost expression on his face. Finally Patti spoke.

"Amy," she said, "Jessica and her father are used to going on overnight hikes together. I think they'd like to get away alone."

"That's not fair!" Her whining got louder; she was working on a tear.

"Look, Amy!" Patti said crossly. "You don't think anything is fair unless it is your idea. Besides, you could never keep up with the two of them on a hike."

"I want to go," Amy said stubbornly.

Dad put his hand over Patti's. "Maybe we shouldn't go just now."

No! I cried inside. *Don't take this away from me!*

"Anyway," my father continued, "I hate to leave you two alone on the boat."

"We'll be fine," Patti told him. "What could happen?"

"Well..." Dad looked back up the mountain. "I don't know."

Please Dad! I kept saying in my head. *Please!* Maybe I should have said it out loud. Instead, I gave him *the look*.

Amy whimpered. Her lower lip trembled. "I'd be so-oo scared," she said. And there it was, one big sloppy tear. This kid should be in movies.

"I tell you what." Dad turned to me. "Why don't you and I just take a day hike? You know, get up early tomorrow morning, pack a lunch and see how far we can get?"

I shrugged. "Sure Dad, whatever."

Amy smiled.

Tears, two. *The look*, no score.

I carried my sketchbook around the deck and sat on the bow with my legs dangling over the water. I opened the sketchbook to my letter to Sara. On it I drew a picture of

Amy being strangled by two huge hands. Her tongue hung out to one side, her eyes were crossed. Underneath I printed, The Brat.

I'm telling you Sara, it's either Amy or me. One of us has got to go!

You think you've got it bad with two little brothers and a sister? What do you say to a trade?

Dad and I almost got to go on an overnight hike, but Amy ruined it. Dad suggested a day hike, but I'm not sure if I want to go at all now.

And here I am behaving myself, trying my best not to be rude or obnoxious. What a drag!

Hot sun beat down on the boat. There wasn't a breath of wind. I went inside, hid the sketchbook under my bunk and changed into my swimsuit. I dove off the stern into clear warm water. As I swam I thought about the hiking trip.

Later, when I climbed out onto the swim grid, I had made up my mind. One day was better than nothing.

That afternoon we all piled into the dinghy for a tour of the inlet. By the time we got back a wind had come up. It turned the water choppy and grew stronger by the hour. In the late afternoon Dad and Patti listened to the marine broadcast on the VHF radio. It predicted gale force winds on the water overnight and all the next day.

Already the boat was rocking back and forth. Dad and Patti rechecked the ropes to be sure they would hold. Then Dad sat down beside me. "Jess," he began. "I don't think tomorrow would be a good day to go hiking."

"Why not?"

He scratched his head and looked across the water where the waves were building. "I don't like to leave the boat in this wind. I'm not sure the anchor will hold."

"You mean you don't like to leave Patti and Amy," I snapped.

He put his hand on my shoulder. He wasn't angry; he simply looked sad. "I wouldn't feel right about it," he said. "Sorry, Jess, but we'll go another time. I promise."

I pulled away from him. I needed to be alone, but that was impossible on this stupid boat. So I got my sketchbook and rowed the dinghy to shore. I walked across the beach to the river. Using small rocks as stepping-stones, I made my way to a big, smooth boulder in the middle of the river. I sat there with water rushing all around me and roaring in my ears.

Alone at last.

I stayed on that rock for hours, sketching and thinking. I tried to draw Sara's face but couldn't get it right, so I added to my letter instead. Not that Sara will ever get to read it because where could I mail it? There was no way to reach Sara. The cell phone didn't work with all those mountains around and there was no way to send an e-mail.

So anyway, Amy wins again. No hike. Big surprise.

If only you were here, we could go hiking together and forget about our problems for a while. It's so beautiful up here, I could almost be happy. If only we had two less people along.

By the time I rowed back to the boat I had made a decision.

At dinner I told them about it.

"You're not going!" Dad said, shovelling in a mouthful of stew.

"Why not?" I pushed my plate away and glared at him. "I can take care of myself."

"Oh yeah?" Amy piped up.

"Amy," Patti told her. "You stay out of this."

"It's too dangerous to go hiking alone," Dad said. "And overnight is out of the question. You don't have enough experience. You might fall and get hurt. How would anyone find you?"

Wow! He had a ready-made list. What could I say? Nothing, so I gave him *the look*. It wasn't a huge success since he was staring out the window.

"This isn't an island, you know," he went on. "It's the mainland. Grizzly country. I saw signs of bear near the river today."

"So? It was grizzly country where we hiked last year. They never bothered us. Besides, I'm not afraid of bears."

"Then you're a fool!" He leaned back in his seat and glared at me.

"That's not fair," Patti said. "Jessica isn't a fool."

"Yes she is," Amy said.

"Amy! Either keep your mouth shut or get out of here," Dad snapped.

I grinned. They were both getting mad at Amy instead of me. But Amy knew how to handle it.

She looked up with a lost, frightened expression. "There's nowhere to go!" she cried.

I groaned.

"Just be quiet," Dad growled.

Tears, not so good. *The look*, worse.

It was my turn to do the dishes. Everyone else was sitting on the back deck. Dad and Patti were playing cards. Amy was reading.

I took my time drying the dishes. I kept thinking about being up on the mountain, alone.

Suddenly I knew what I had to do. Dad told me I couldn't go on an overnight hike. Okay, I could accept that.

But he didn't forbid a day hike.

I found two bagels, spread peanut butter on them, and wrapped them in waxed paper. Then I grabbed a handful of trail mix and stuck it in a plastic bag.

I glanced outside. Amy was staring at me over top of her book. Her eyes darted back to the page.

I got some candies and two chocolate bars and stuffed everything into a paper bag. Then I dragged my backpack out from under my bunk. I shoved in a pair of jeans, a sweatshirt, my sketchbook and my lunch.

"What're you doing?"

I jumped. Amy was right behind me.

"Don't sneak up on me," I snapped. But I wondered how much she had seen.

"Why would I want to sneak up on you?" She looked from me to my backpack with a strange expression on her face. Then she reached over me to get a book from the shelf behind her bunk. "I can't stand even looking at your bunk," she said. "How come you're so messy?"

"How come you're such a brat?"

I couldn't stand looking at her bunk either. Her sleeping bag was always smoothed out, perfectly neat. All her stuff was carefully put away on the shelf. It just wasn't natural.

That night I went to bed early. I wanted to be up by 5:30, but I didn't dare set the alarm on my watch. I lay awake for hours, staring into the darkness.

Suddenly I jerked awake. Little cracks of light crept around the heavy curtains. In the darkness I grabbed my watch, but it was too dark inside to read the time. I pushed one of the little buttons and the alarm beeped. *Crap.*

I tried another button. The face lit up. It was 5:47. Time to go. Now or never.

I wriggled into the clothes I had laid at the foot of my bunk. I reached for my backpack. Amy moaned and rustled around in her bunk above my head.

Two bare feet swung down in front of my face.

chapter seven

I froze.

Amy slid to the floor and wandered toward the bathroom. Waves slapped against the hull. Dad's snores rattled the door to the V-berth in the bow. That was good; at least someone was asleep.

Amy came back and climbed up to her bunk. I lay very still, listening. I had the feeling Amy was listening back.

Time slipped away; I had to make my move. I got up, grabbed my backpack and tiptoed through the darkened boat.

Outside, behind the boat, the dinghy bobbed up and down on choppy waves. I climbed onto the swim grid and grabbed the rope to pull the dinghy close. I stashed my backpack and started to climb in.

A hand touched my shoulder. I almost fell overboard.

I looked up. "What are you doing here, Amy?"

"I'm coming with you," she whispered.

She was dressed just like me, in jeans, a jacket and running shoes. But on top of her head was that stupid pink scrunchy and on her back she carried a bright pink knapsack.

"Oh, no you're not!"

"Yes," she said, "I am." She climbed over the stern to get into the dinghy.

"Don't you understand?" I spat the words at her. "I don't want you. If I have to spend all day looking out for you, I'll never get anywhere."

"Nobody needs to look out for me. I can take care of myself."

"Right. Tears aren't going to work if we meet up with a bear."

"We won't," she said. "You're just trying to scare me." She climbed into the dinghy and sat down. "Besides, if I don't go, you don't go. I'll call Dad."

"Your dad isn't here, he left you, remember? And I don't blame him, I bet you drove him crazy!" As soon as the words left my mouth I was sorry.

This time Amy wasn't acting. Her whole body sagged. She lowered her head and stared down at her hands.

"Oh, all right, you can come." *Crap! Did I really say that? The Brat wins again.*

There was no sly little smile this time. Amy sat on the stern seat and hung her head while I rowed. When we hit the beach she brushed away a couple of tears before she climbed out.

While I tied up the dinghy Amy started across the beach. She walked quickly, taking big steps and holding her head high. I ran after her. She crouched beside the river and splashed water on her face.

"Amy!" The roar of rushing water took my voice away. I scrambled over the rocks.

She started up the river.

"Amy!" I called again.

I finally caught up and put my hand on her shoulder. "I'm sorry," I said.

"It doesn't matter." Her face was as pink as her scrunchy and her eyes watered. She turned away.

"Look," I said, "will you wait for me? You can't just go charging up the river without knowing what you're doing."

"Why not?" She looked surprised.

"You've got to read the river," I told her.

She looked at me as if I had gone nuts. She knew how to read books. But rivers?

"Look over there," I pointed to the far side of the river. "Do you think we could walk over there?"

Trees and thick undergrowth grew to the river's edge. Tangled branches reached out over the water.

"Of course not," she said. "But we don't need to, there's lots of room on this side." She started walking again, shaking her head.

I walked beside her. "When the river floods in spring these rocks we're walking on are underwater. That's why there's nothing growing here."

"So?"

"So the river twists and turns all the way down the mountain. Every time we go around a bend things will change. We'll have to cross back and forth almost as often as the river turns."

"How?"

"You'll see."

Sure enough, around the first bend the gravel bar we were walking on narrowed and disappeared. Thick bushes blocked our way. But on the opposite side there was a space wide enough to walk beside the river.

I stopped and studied the river, looking for the safest place to cross. Amy followed me to the water's edge where it was only about four meters across. Like most mountain streams this one had boulders here and there sticking high and dry out of the water. You can nearly always find some to use as stepping-stones. There were two here, evenly spaced and big enough to land on with two feet. White water rushed around them.

"We'll cross on those rocks," I said, pointing at them.

"No way!"

"It's easy," I told her. "Anyone can do it. No problem."

"I can't," she whined.

"Do you want to go back?" I hoped she would say yes. Then I could go on alone.

"No," she said stubbornly.

"Then follow me." I leapt onto the first boulder, jumped to the second one and landed on the far side of the river. I turned around.

Amy stood on the gravel bar where I had left her. She stared at the first boulder. She looked very small.

I waited. She bent her knees, wiggled her feet, ready to jump ... and stepped back. Two blue eyes looked at me helplessly.

"I can't wait forever," I called.

She tried again. And she chickened out again.

"I think you should go back to the boat," I called.

She gave me a quick angry glance and jumped. She landed squarely on the first boulder and leapt to the next one. Then she was beside me, grinning as if she'd just climbed Mount Everest.

"See? I told you it was easy," I said.

We walked in silence to the next bend in the river. There we had to cross over again, but this time Amy didn't hesitate.

"I wish my father could see me now," she said.

"Why?"

"He thinks I can't do anything but read... and, you know, do girl stuff."

"Big surprise," I said.

She shrugged. "He never took me hiking or anything like that. He said I would slow him down."

I stopped and stared down at her. "But I thought he spoiled you rotten!"

She glanced at me and turned away. "He bought me stuff," she said. "As long as I kept out of his way and got straight *A*'s at school."

"Harsh," I said. *No wonder she's so weird!*

chapter eight

The sun rose higher in the sky. The cool morning grew warm and then hot. At the bottom of a steep waterfall we stopped to take off our jackets and stuff them into our packs. Here the river had changed again. It was narrow and very deep with sheer rock cliffs rising straight up on both sides.

"What do we do now?" Amy asked.

"We climb."

Amy stared up at the wall of rock. She looked down at the rushing water. Her face turned green.

"Scared?" I asked.

"Of course not. Let's go!"

I scanned the rock cliff for grooves to use as handholds and toeholds. I traced a good route to the top, one Amy could handle if she didn't panic. But I have to admit I was scared. Not for me, but for Amy. I wasn't sure she could do it. Not that it was a difficult climb. It wasn't very high, it was good solid rock, and there were tons of places to hang on with feet and hands. But Amy was so helpless.

"I'm not sure you should, Amy," I told her.

Her eyes narrowed. "Are you trying to get rid of me?"

"No," I grinned, "not really. I just don't want you to fall. We can turn back now if you want. Maybe we can find an easier route."

"I can do it," she insisted. To prove it she started climbing up the rock cliff like she had been doing it all her life. She even followed the route I would have taken.

"Slow down!" I called, climbing up behind. Either she didn't hear or she didn't listen.

Amy had almost reached the top when she got into trouble. She veered off the easy route and tried to climb straight up.

"Not that way, Amy!" I scrambled to catch up. When I looked next she was pressed against the cliff above me with her toes balanced in a tiny cleft in the rock face. Her fingers clung to the rocks above her head.

"What's wrong?" I called.

"Nothing!"

"Then why don't you move?"

She didn't answer. She moved one foot, trying to gain a higher foothold on the rock. She was so close the toe of her running shoe touched a dry alder leaf that hung there. But she couldn't quite make it.

She pulled back. The leaf came loose and floated past my nose.

"You should have let me go first," I yelled.

"Jess? I'm scared."

I looked down. The alder leaf landed gently on the fast moving water and was swept away. It disappeared over the waterfall.

My heart pounded in my ears. "Keep still," I called. "I'll climb above you and pull you up."

Amy pressed her cheek against the rock. Her whole skinny body was squashed against the rock face like a bug on a windshield. Her legs started to tremble. With the effort of balancing on her toes, she wouldn't last much longer.

I needed to get to the top. And fast. Above and to my right Amy blocked the easy route. Straight above my head the cliff was smooth and shiny. To the left didn't look much better.

"Amy!" I called, "I need to climb back down and find another way up."

She didn't say a word, but I heard a soft whimper. Her legs were shaking badly; there was no time to lose.

I knew she couldn't hang on long enough for me to go down and climb back up again, so I had to take a chance. I studied the rock above, on the left side, and spotted something I had missed before. A sturdy tree root hung over top of the cliff. If only I could reach it...

I dug my fingers into any cleft or groove I could find and pulled with all my strength. My toes fumbled for footholds. My feet found a narrow ledge, solid enough to hold my weight. My fingers curled around an uneven chunk of rock. The root was just above my head. I reached for it.

I felt the rough bark with my fingertips but couldn't get my hand around it. Just a few more inches.

By this time I was breathing heavily and was so hot I felt faint. Sweat poured down my forehead. I heard a groan from Amy. From the corner of my eye, I caught a movement. My heart stopped. Some small rocks bounced down the cliff and splashed into the river below.

"Hang on, Amy! I'm almost there!"

My backpack was weighing me down. I had to get rid of it. If I slid it straight down the cliff face it should land on the rocks below and not fall into the water.

I let it slip from my shoulders until I held it in my left hand. I lowered it as far as possible, against the cliff, down by my feet. Then I let go. It landed on the rocks with a thud.

"JESSICA!" Amy screamed.

"I'm all right," I called. "It's just my backpack."

Free of the backpack, I felt like I could do anything. I pushed up on tiptoes and stretched my legs, my arms and my fingers until I could wrap my hands around the tree root. It was a living root, strong and healthy. Pulling, grasping and climbing with my toes like a goat, I managed to get the top half of my body over the cliff edge. The rest was easy.

"I'm up!" I yelled. "I'll be there in a second."

The undergrowth at the top of the cliff was thick and scratchy. I held my hands in front of my face and pushed my way through, but by then I couldn't tell where Amy was.

"Amy?" I yelled.

There was no answer.

"Amy. Talk to me. Help me find you."

"I'm here." Her frightened voice was right below my feet.

Cautiously, clinging to a tree trunk for support, I peeked over the edge. And there was that pink scrunchy. What a beautiful sight.

Pushing aside thick bushes, I lay down and threw one arm over the edge. If only I had thought to bring some rope. But it was too late for that. I reached for her wrist. Found it. Grabbed it. She clung on like a leech. But I couldn't lift her.

"Amy," I tried to sound calm, shouting over the river noise. "You've got to help me here. Pull with your free hand and push with your toes. You've got to find that next foothold."

"I can't!" she screamed.

"Amy, screaming is a waste of energy. You can do it. You have to."

Her hand trembled in mine. I needed to get her moving

"Okay, Amy. Take a deep breath. On three I start to pull." I didn't dare give her time to think. "One, two, three..."

Flat on my stomach with my feet wrapped around bushes behind, I pulled with all my strength. She must have helped because soon I could reach her other wrist. I inched my way backward, pulling her with me.

At last she was safe, lying on the trampled bushes, panting for air. She stared at me with frightened eyes.

I sat up, shaking all over. Neither of us spoke.

chapter nine

After a while Amy sat up too. Her eyes had a dazed look. Her face was white as milk and her bottom lip quivered. "You saved my life," she whispered.

"No," I said, trying to cheer her up. "You would have been all right."

She shook her head. "I was so scared." She looked down at her trembling hands. "I guess my father was right."

"Don't be dumb," I said. "You got stuck in a bad spot; it could happen to anyone."

To change the subject I asked, "How about some food? I brought bagels and..." That's when I remembered my pack at the bottom of the cliff.

But Amy took off her knapsack and started fishing around in it. She pulled out two oranges and a plastic bag full of muffins. They were squashed and broken, but we didn't care. We wolfed them down.

"When did you pack these?" I asked through a mouthful.

"I, uh, oh..." She studied her fingernails. "Last night."

"So you *were* spying on me, you little brat!"

Her head jerked back as if I had punched her. She looked away. "I didn't mean to, I just looked up when you were wrapping those bagels, then I saw you pack some clothes and I figured it out. I wanted to come with you."

"Why?"

Amy still didn't look at me. She bit into her orange and the juice ran down her chin.

"I thought it would be fun." She wiped her chin with the back of her hand. In a small voice she added, "I thought you might start to like me."

I almost choked on my orange. "I didn't know you wanted me to like you."

She looked at me then, her eyes wide. "Of course I do," she said. Then she turned away again. "I just don't know how."

"Well," I said, "you could start by not being such a jerk when my dad and Patti are around."

She glanced at me sideways. "I can't seem to help it," she admitted. "I want them to like me too."

"Of course they like you. You get good grades, you always wear the right clothes, you're insanely neat and, even more important, you never give them *the look*." I rolled my eyes.

Amy grinned. "But they still like you better. You're good at everything and I'm—well—hopeless."

I snorted and got to my feet. "That's sure not the way I see it."

Amy stood up too and brushed leaves and twigs from her jeans.

"I guess you want to turn back now?" I asked.

"Are you kidding? I want to find that lake!"

Suddenly I felt very old and disgustingly responsible. "But my dad and your mother will be worried."

"No they won't. I left them a note. It said I went with you and we'd be gone for the whole day." She smiled, quite pleased with herself.

"You did? So you just assumed I'd let you come?"

Her smile went crooked.

"Okay, listen, Amy," I said honestly. "I just don't think you can do it. I've got to climb down anyway to get my backpack. I'll help you down the cliff and then you can follow the stream back to the boat."

Amy's face turned a lovely shade of green.

"Or, I can go with you." *Shoot! Did I say that?*

"You can't make me go back!" She picked up her knapsack and glared at me stubbornly.

I gave her *the look*, but of course it didn't work on Amy. She was right, like it or not, I was stuck with her. "Wait here," I ordered and started back down the cliff for my pack.

We climbed for hours, and I was so hungry my stomach ached, but I didn't want to be the first to stop. Besides, I kept thinking that around the next bend we would suddenly come upon the lake.

We climbed up some rocks beside a low waterfall. At the top we had to cross the river again. It was a difficult jump, from a steep rock across fast-moving water.

"Maybe we should turn back," I suggested. "We've come a long way."

"You're not getting rid of me that easily!" Before I could stop her, Amy jumped. She landed on the far side and swung around with a huge grin on her face. "It's easy," she said. "Need some help?"

I jumped across.

We hadn't gone much farther when Amy said she was hungry.

"Okay," I told her, "around the next bend we'll stop and eat."

We got a drink from the river and sat on some flat rocks. I took out the bagels and trail mix.

"What's this?" Amy asked.

She pointed at something dark and sticky-looking on the rock beside her. I looked more closely and saw berry seeds in it. I knew exactly what it was, but I didn't want to scare Amy. Who knew what she might do?

"What is it?" she insisted.

"Nothing."

"Don't tell me it's nothing, I'm not that stupid. Is it from a cougar?"

"No, just a bear."

"Crap!" She jumped to her feet.

I glanced up in surprise. That was the first time I'd heard Amy use a word like *crap*. If Dad ever heard her, he would probably say I had corrupted sweet little Amy. "Yes, it definitely is," I grinned, "but, don't worry. It's not fresh poop."

"Let's go," Amy said.

"I thought you were hungry."

"Not anymore."

"Look," I said calmly. "The bear could be anywhere by now. It could be ahead of us, it could be watching us from the forest. As long as we don't surprise it, it shouldn't bother us."

But Amy refused to sit down. "I'm going," she said and started off.

I groaned and shoved everything back into my backpack. I wished Sara were here instead of this stubborn kid. Sara could take care of herself, she loved to hike in the mountains and she wasn't afraid of a little bear poop.

The river got smaller and smaller until it was no more than a little creek. Bushes crowded in on both sides and there was no clear land at all. But we didn't want to quit, so we waded in, shoes and all. The shallow water was so cold it made my ankles hurt.

In front of me Amy climbed out at a small muddy spot and started rubbing her ankles. My shoes squished into soft mud as I waded over to join her.

"Look!" she said, her voice hushed.

Sunk deeply into the mud was the biggest bear print I had ever seen. It was so clear you could count all five of its toes. The bear's long slender claws showed too, and they pointed toward the bushes. A pathway of broken branches and trampled bushes led away from the stream. "It's a grizzly," I said. "I think we should turn back right now."

"No way!" Amy shook her head stubbornly. "I'm not quitting until we find that lake!"

"All right," I said. I really wanted to find the lake too. We had come so far and I figured we were almost there now. I checked my watch. "But if we don't find it in half an hour we turn back. Agreed?"

Amy pressed her lips together, then she nodded. "Okay."

Around the next bend we saw it. Smooth, blue water shining in sunlight. We waded toward it.

At the lake's edge we stopped. It wasn't a big lake—not much more than a pond, really. But it was beautiful. It was surrounded by green, forested hills that swooped down to the water's edge. At the far end, peaking above the valley between two hills, a rugged, snow-capped mountain rose up to the sky. Its mirror image on the water was as clear as the mountain itself. The laughing cry of a loon echoed across the lake.

A fallen log lay half in the water where the lake emptied into the creek. We waded to the log, took off our backpacks and laid them on it. Then we took off our shoes and socks and put them in the hot sun. Mud squished between my toes in the shallow water. It felt good, but the water was cold, like the river. I wanted to get out.

On the far side of the log was a grassy area and I started toward it. Suddenly a shower of cold water hit me across the back. Amy laughed. I swung around and glared at her.

She went as pink as that stupid scrunchy that hung loosely from her messed-up hair. Quick as a flash I bent down and sent a spray of water into her face. She came at me like a windmill, flinging water with her arms and legs.

In the end I'm not sure who got the worst of it. We were both soaked when we staggered out, laughing, onto the grass.

Amy lay back in the sunshine, complaining about blisters on her feet. So I got out the first-aid kit. Dad always insisted I take it in my backpack, even on a short hike, and that day I was glad. I stuck Band-Aids on Amy's blisters. My feet were sore too, so I stuck a few Band-Aids on the worst blisters.

We each gobbled down a bagel and a chocolate bar. We saved the trail mix for later. Amy lay back again and closed her eyes. I pulled my sketchbook from my pack and flipped it open. But my eyelids were heavy and the sun shone warm on my face. My head drooped.

I heard a gasp. My head jerked up. Amy sat beside me, staring at my sketchbook, her eyes huge, her face white as death.

I looked down. There was my drawing of Amy being strangled. *The Brat* was printed in big letters and the sentence underneath said: *I'm telling you Sara, it's either Amy or me. One of us has got to go!*

Her eyes turned to my face. "You want to get rid of me!" she whispered.

"No, Amy, of course not! I was just, you know, mad at you when I wrote that yesterday. You ruined my hike with Dad."

"So, are you planning to leave me up here?"

"Yeah, right, Amy. I'm going to take off and leave you to the bears."

She jumped to her feet and picked up her knapsack. Her eyes went all watery, like she was going to cry.

"Listen, Amy, if I wanted to get rid of you, why would I have helped you up the cliff? You said yourself that I saved your life."

She looked uncertain.

"Besides," I grinned, "you're not nearly as bad as I thought you were."

"Thanks heaps," she said and grinned back at me.

I glanced at my watch. "It's getting late. We need to get moving."

Amy groaned.

chapter ten

We had no trouble wading back through the slow moving part of the river. The cold water felt good on our sore feet.

But soon the river began to spill over rocks as it twisted its way down the mountainside. We had to start crossing back and forth again. After a whole day of it, jumping from rock to rock gets very hard on the legs. Mine were tired and aching, so I knew how Amy must feel. And the blisters didn't help either.

Amy dragged her feet as if they were made of lead. But she didn't complain, not once. When we got back to the bear dropping, she stepped over it like it wasn't even there.

The shadows of the tall evergreens crept across the river. I knew then that we should have turned back a lot earlier, but I hadn't counted on Amy being so tired. The air had cooled down quickly and we stopped to put on our jackets.

Amy jumped onto a flat rock in the middle of the river. All at once her legs gave out under her. She stumbled and fell sideways.

"You okay?" I called.

She sat up. "I need a rest," she begged. "Just a few minutes. Please?"

I shook my head. I knew her leg muscles would seize up if she rested now, so I had to keep her moving.

"It's getting late," I said. "We've got to get down the mountain before dark."

"I don't care." She whined, then caught herself. She looked up at me shyly, "I'm so tired."

Her shoes were wet, her jeans were soaked from the knees down, her hair was a tangled mess and that stupid scrunchy still clung crookedly on top. She looked so pathetic I almost gave in but I didn't dare. "You do realize that bears usually come down to the river at dusk?" I asked.

She made a sad little noise in her throat and pushed herself up. "Okay, you win. I'm coming."

We stopped above the small waterfall where Amy had easily jumped across earlier. Water rushed through a narrow gorge between two large rocks. The rock on the far side was so steep it would not be easy to land on, but we had no choice.

"I can't do it!" Amy said. "I'm too tired."

"Of course you can," I told her confidently. "Watch me."

I didn't waste any time. I gathered my strength and pushed off, leaping over the fast water. One foot landed on the rock, the other slid into the water. I grabbed the pointed top of the rock and pulled myself to safety.

"See?" I called. "It's easy. Throw me your knapsack."

I caught her knapsack and put both packs on the rocks out of the way. Then I turned back to help Amy. "Your turn!"

She looked at me. She looked over the waterfall to the rocks below. She looked down at the water rushing between us and then back at me again.

"I'm right here." I held on with one hand and leaned forward to stretch my other hand toward her. "I'll help you."

She shook her head.

"Jump!" I yelled.

Amy hesitated. She took a deep breath, stepped back and jumped.

Her feet hit the rock and slid backward into the water. I reached for her. She grabbed at my hand, and our fingers touched. I almost had her, but she slipped away.

I threw myself down on the rock and reached for her hands. But it was too late. Amy was in the water. Her long hair floated on the surface; I made a grab for it. I touched it but couldn't hang on.

"AMY!" I screamed.

Her big blue eyes stared at me helplessly before she disappeared over the edge. I scrambled to my feet. There was something in my hand. I looked down and saw her pink scrunchy. *Oh, Amy.*

"Let her be all right! Let her be all right!" I said over and over as I climbed down the rocks beside the waterfall.

I hit level ground and scrambled over loose rocks toward the river's edge. Then I saw her. Downstream, pushed up against a log at the edge of a shallow pool, she lay half in, half out of the water. One leg stuck out at a weird angle. Her arms were bent beneath her and her face lay against a rock. She didn't move.

I hurried over and crouched beside her. I gently touched her shoulder. She moaned.

"You're alive!" I cried. I didn't think it was possible the way she looked.

"I think so." Her voice was tiny and her face was still pressed up against the rock.

"We need to get you out of the water."

I tried to take her arms and help her move, but she cried out in pain. The fingers of one hand dug into the flesh of my wrist. Her other hand hung limply at the end of a twisted arm.

"I can't," she whispered.

"Listen," I spoke sternly. "I know how much it hurts, but you've got to get out of this cold water. Do you understand?"

She moaned.

"Amy, you're a brave kid. I know that now. So just try to hang on and I'll carry you. Okay?"

She nodded.

I bent down and slid one arm under her stomach. I put my other arm under the leg that looked normal. Gently I began to lift. Amy gasped and went limp all over. She was unconscious. Maybe that was good because it saved her some pain as I half carried, half dragged her from the water to a smooth, sandy patch of ground.

She looked so small lying there, all wet and shivering. Not moving. My stomach twisted in knots. My mind whirled. I wished Dad was with us because he would know what to do.

Okay. I told myself, it's up to you. Do something. I took a deep breath and tried to think. Babysitting. First aid. I took a course when I was twelve. What to do?

Don't move the patient. Well, I couldn't have left her in the water.

Check her heartbeat and breathing. Okay, that part of her was working fine. But her leg! Her arm! I couldn't fix them.

And she was shivering. I couldn't leave her to go for help until she was warm.

I went back to get our packs. My fingers shook as I fumbled for my first-aid kit. I took out the scissors and started cutting up the leg of Amy's soggy jeans. I prayed she wouldn't wake up until I had finished.

I moved her slightly to get the jeans off. Amy winced and her eyes opened, just a slit. She looked at her mangled jeans and her eyes got big. "What do you think you're doing?" She sounded like the old Amy.

"You won't need any jeans if we don't get you dry," I snapped.

She grinned. Or maybe it was a wince. "My favorite jeans," she whispered.

I pulled out the spare clothes I always carry in case of emergency. But I had to cut one leg of my jeans to get them over her broken leg. "*My* favorite jeans," I said as I ruined them forever.

When she had on dry jeans, and my dry sweatshirt and jacket, I climbed up to the bushes above the river. I came back with an armful of dry leaves, twigs and pieces of wood.

I grabbed my sketchbook and ripped out a few empty pages and one full one. "Look, Amy," I said, "I'm getting rid of that letter to Sara. No one will ever see it."

I scrunched up the papers and placed dry leaves and twigs on top. Using matches from the first-aid kit, I lit the paper on fire. Slowly I began feeding the little fire with more twigs. When it was big enough I put on one chunk of wood and then another.

Amy wriggled closer, trying to get warm.

chapter eleven

The temperature kept dropping. The fire was hot, but a breeze crept up from behind, and Amy couldn't stop shivering. I thought about the hot-water bottles on the boat. That gave me an idea.

The rocks near the fire were warm. I propped some against Amy's back and gave her one to hold close against her stomach. She held it with her good arm and wrapped herself around it.

When they cooled I replaced them. "Are you warm now?" I asked.

She nodded.

"Hungry?"

"No."

"I need to go for help."

"NO!" she cried, and winced in pain. "Don't leave me!"

"I have to Amy. You need help. We can't wait until morning."

"But the bears will get me!"

Oh-oh. Now I was sorry for what I had told her earlier. "Look," I said, "bears hardly ever bother people unless you take them by surprise. And you won't be going anywhere."

But I will, I thought. And it would be dark before I got down.

"You said they come down to the river at night."

"I only said that to keep you going. Anyway, bears are afraid of fire. You just keep that fire burning and they won't come anywhere near."

"Honest?"

"Honest," I said. *I hope.*

I gathered enough wood to last all night and piled it beside Amy. I stuffed the trail mix and all the food wrappers in my pockets, so there would be no hint of food smell near Amy. I tucked my backpack under her head as a pillow. All I needed were the jeans and T-shirt I was wearing. I left everything else with Amy.

"I won't be long," I told her. "You'll see."

She looked up with tears in her eyes. "I'm scared," she said.

"There's nothing to be scared of. Just keep that fire going so we can find you. I'll be back soon. I promise."

I saw her take a deep breath. She tried to smile but winced in pain. "Don't worry," she whispered, "I'll be fine."

My throat tightened. She didn't look fine at all. I patted her hand. "See you soon." I started downriver.

Without Amy I moved a lot faster. My legs were tired and my feet hurt with every step, but without my backpack I felt as light as a deer.

Above the big waterfall I stopped to look down. The light was dim and the river roared below, dark and scary. There was no time to lose. I took a deep breath, gathered my courage and lowered myself over the cliff. I followed the easy route I had checked out that morning when I went down for my backpack.

Halfway down, groping for a foothold, my toe touched a loose rock. It wobbled and shook loose. I held my breath as it bounced down the cliff and splashed into the river. I swallowed and kept going. Slowly. Carefully.

At last I stepped onto the large, flat boulder at the bottom. That's when I heard it. It was a strange sound—somewhere between a grunt and a sigh. So close!

I turned my head just enough to see over my shoulder. My mouth went dry. A chill ran down my spine. Below me was the biggest bear I had seen in my life. Its front paws rested on the boulder, its long, sharp claws were inches away from my foot. Its huge mouth was open so wide the rotten-fish stink of its breath nearly knocked me over.

I didn't move. I could not have moved if I had wanted to. But I pictured myself scrambling over the rocks with that bear loping along behind. It would reach out and flatten me with one swipe of its giant paw. I squeezed my eyes shut.

The bear grunted.

My eyes flew open.

The bear sniffed the air near my feet. I had to keep still. It was my only chance, but it was so hard to do.

The bear moved one giant paw until its needle-sharp claws touched the toe of my shoe. My heart pounded against my ribs. I couldn't breathe. The bear put its face close to my leg, like a near-sighted person reading a book. Its breath felt hot and moist through my jeans as it sniffed up and down my leg.

My heart stopped. Could the bear smell the remains of our lunch? How about the trail mix? I had to get away. I would kick that bear on the end of its soft nose and scramble straight up the cliff. Right. And be squashed flat in two seconds—ripped to shreds in three.

The bear sniffed my wet running shoe and grunted in disgust. It dropped down on all fours, lifted its nose to sniff the air once more, snorted and walked away.

I started breathing again, tiny shallow breaths. But I was afraid to move. I listened to that bear crash over rocks in the direction I needed to go. It tossed rocks aside, looking for mice or voles. A few minutes later, in the darkness of the woods above, I heard a loud crunch like a tree snapping in half.

Still I waited, scared out of my mind. Then I thought of Amy lying by the fire alone, afraid and hurting. I took a deep breath and climbed down from the boulder to continue on my way.

I tried not to look at the frightening shadows under the trees above. Any one of them could be hiding the dark shape of a bear. Once, in a shadow beside a boulder, I was sure something moved. Later, up in the forest, something rustled through the bushes. Something big.

It took me forever to reach the final stretch

of river. Darkness crept toward me from all sides. Then suddenly, dead ahead, something orange and flickering caught my eye. A fire! Dad must be waiting on the beach.

"Dad!" I yelled. "I'm here!" But he couldn't hear. All at once I felt so tired and my feet hurt so much that I wanted to collapse, right where I was. I wanted Dad to find me and help me over the last few meters of rough ground.

I stumbled over the dry riverbed toward the flickering light. "Dad!" But the river was too loud. Then I saw him. He stood by the fire, wearing a backpack and looking up the mountainside. "Dad!"

There was a movement beside me, a light flashed in my eyes and away.

Patti threw her arms around me, and I collapsed against her.

"Thank Heaven you're all right!" she said. "Your dad was about to go looking for you."

It felt good to be comforted by her. For two seconds I felt as if everything *was* all right. But of course it wasn't.

She pulled back. "Where's Amy?"

I swallowed. "Amy's still up there," I said softly, "she's hurt."

Her hands gripped my shoulders. Her voice was a whisper. "What happened?"

chapter twelve

We all piled into the dinghy. On *Fanta-sea*, Dad switched to the Emergency channel of the VHF radio and called the coast guard station at Comox. When he told them about Amy's fire, they promised to send a helicopter right away.

Patti looked worried. "Do you think she'll keep the fire burning?" she asked. "Amy's not very good at things like that."

"You'd be surprised," I told her. I was sure that as long as Amy was awake she would keep that fire going.

Dad rowed back to the beach to keep his own signal fire going. While I took off my wet shoes and changed into dry clothes, Patti made me a pot of hot tea and a thick chicken sandwich. I was so tired I didn't think I could eat, but I wolfed the food down and drank a mug of tea.

Patti couldn't sit still. She paced back and forth and looked out into the night. We listened to the crackle of the VHF radio and hoped for the sound of a helicopter. Patti went outside to stand on the back deck.

I poured two mugs of tea and took them out. I handed one to Patti and she took it, but I'm not sure if she even noticed.

"Amy's so helpless," she said suddenly.

"Not so much as you think," I told her.

"She always tried so hard to impress her father," Patti went on. "But it never worked. He only wanted her to keep quiet and behave herself."

Patti talked about her ex-husband as if he was dead.

"She loves her dad," I said.

"I guess," Patti said. "But he hurt her so badly that she wants nothing to do with him right now. She won't even talk to him when he phones."

We looked up at the black outline of the mountain against a starry sky. It was so huge and Amy was so small.

"That's why she wants to call your father Dad," Patti said. "She really needs a father right now."

"Uh," I grunted.

"Jess, I know how much you must miss your mom."

Where did that come from?

"You always will," Patti said, "for the rest of your life."

When I said nothing she went on, "I understand that, Jessica, and I want you to know I would never try to take her place."

I grunted.

"And I don't expect you to call me Mom. Patti suits me just fine."

My throat was tight and aching. All I could do was nod.

"Do you hear that?" Patti asked.

I listened. In the distance was the thump-thump-thump of rotors.

"Do you want to go back to the beach?" I asked.

"Yes!"

I called Dad and stuffed my feet back into my wet shoes. When Dad rowed us back to shore we saw a light in the sky, growing brighter and brighter. We reached the beach and the helicopter hovered above us, so loud I couldn't think. It flooded us with light.

Patti jumped up and down and waved her arms. She pointed upriver. I couldn't believe it when they started lowering someone. A dark shape swung below the big machine and finally touched down on the beach. A man's voice shouted, "Which one of you can help us locate the girl?"

I guessed it was up to me. I looked at Patti. She nodded but couldn't speak. My dad put his hand on my shoulder and walked over with me.

"I'm Mike," the man said. "I'll help you into the horse collar."

A few minutes later I was swinging through the night air, held by a big strap under my arms. I was facing Mike, whose harness was somehow hooked to mine.

I looked down. Dad's fire looked so small and far away I was surprised they had spotted it. I should have been scared out of my mind, but everything happened so fast I didn't have time to think.

A man and woman helped us into the big yellow helicopter. They told me to sit near the pilot and co-pilot.

"Hi," the pilot had a friendly smile, "I'm Anne. We need you to look down and try to pinpoint the exact spot where you left your friend."

"She's not my friend."

The pilot looked surprised.

"She's Amy, my, uh...sister."

Anne nodded.

"And if you follow the river, we should see Amy's fire."

The searchlight guided us up the river. I

stared down, searching for the small glow of a signal fire. I recognized the high waterfall where Amy had been stuck. But everything looked different from up here. It was hard to tell a waterfall from rapids. And we moved so fast I lost track of where we were.

The searchlight fell on the lake. My heart clenched. We had missed her. "Don't worry," Anne said. "I'll take us down a little closer to the ground."

We headed downriver. Before I knew it we were back at the waterfall.

"Okay," I swallowed and tried to stay calm, "we need to concentrate on the top half of the river. I'm sure that's where she is."

"And you're certain she has a fire going?"

"Yes, I'm—almost sure."

"Then let's try turning out the searchlight. The fire will show up better that way."

It worked. At last I spotted a tiny red glow and knew we had found Amy.

Mike and the woman who had helped me aboard went down on ropes. Two other people lowered a stretcher.

We hovered over the spot, but I couldn't tell what was happening below.

"Don't worry," Anne said. "They are both trained paramedics."

"She's coming up!" someone called.

I could see the stretcher swinging in space, but I couldn't make out Amy. It wasn't until they hauled the stretcher on board that I saw her. She looked tiny and her skin was milky white against the blankets.

"Jess," her voice was slurred. Her thin fingers reached up.

I took hold of her hand. "I'm here," I said. "You did great!"

I'm sure she smiled before she winced in pain.

The co-pilot picked up his radio to call in. "We've got the girl," he said. "We're taking her to the hospital in Powell River. Call the *Fanta-sea* and let her parents know."

chapter thirteen

At the hospital they wheeled Amy away.

A nurse with a clipboard came up to me. "I'll need some information," she said.

I stared at her dizzily. Was she swaying back and forth or was it me?

"Come, sit down." The nurse put an arm around my shoulders and guided me to chair. "You're limping!" she said.

"I am?"

How could I not have noticed? It felt as if there were sharp little pebbles in my shoes.

She took off my shoes and put them aside. My feet were a mass of blisters.

"How did you get so wet?"

"We had to walk through the water."

"Wet socks and running shoes," she said. "They'll do it every time!"

After she patched me up the nurse found a quiet waiting room with a couch. I half remember her putting a warm blanket over me before I fell asleep.

"Jess," said a voice above my head. I felt a hand on my shoulder. "Jess!"

"Dad?" I yawned. How did he get here so fast? I tried to ask but could only mumble. My eyes refused to open.

"We just got here," Dad said. "We brought the boat around, but it was so dark on the water we couldn't go very fast."

I forced my eyes open and looked up at his tired face. I blinked toward a window at a pale blue sky. "It's morning already," I said stupidly.

Dad nodded, "It's just past dawn."

He sat beside me. "Amy is going to be fine. Patti is with her now."

"Can I see her?"

"I don't see why not." He stood and took my hands to help me up.

My poor feet! They hurt so much I hobbled down the hall like an old woman.

Weak sunlight spilled into Amy's room. She lay on a high narrow bed and had casts on one leg and one arm. She looked pale and fragile in that early morning light. When she saw me a smile crept across her face.

"Thanks Jess," she mumbled, her voice heavy with sleep.

Dad squeezed Amy's hand. "You're a lucky girl," he said.

Patti started to cry. She bent and kissed Amy's forehead.

"Come on, Jess," Dad said. "Let's leave these two alone. I'll buy you some breakfast."

In the coffee shop I ordered a cinnamon bun and hot chocolate with whipped cream. The hot chocolate went down so good that I asked for another one.

Dad didn't say a word; he just sipped his coffee and stared at his hands. Finally he said, "Jess, I'm really proud of you."

"Anyone would have done the same thing," I told him, embarrassed.

He looked at me then. "I don't just mean last night," he said, "I mean all the time. I'm proud that you are my daughter." He studied his hands again. "I guess I don't show it very well these days."

I stared into my hot chocolate. "So? What's to be proud of? I don't get good grades like Amy. I'm not pretty like Amy. And, you may have noticed, I'm not the neatest person in the world."

He laughed and rolled his eyes. Then he turned serious. "I didn't get good grades either," he admitted. "But you're a good person, Jess, you care about people. And I bet you know more about the outdoors than anyone else your age."

He put his hand over mine. "As for being pretty like Amy, why should you look like her? You look like your mother—so much that sometimes it hurts when I look at you."

I gulped some hot chocolate. It burned in my throat. "I'm sorry," I gasped.

"No, Jess. Don't be sorry. Be proud. Your mother was a wonderful beautiful woman and we will always miss her." He sipped his coffee and put the mug down. "You know, Jess, she loved you very much."

He paused then, as if he wanted to say something else but didn't know how. "And I do too," he added quietly.

"In that case," I said, before he got too mushy, "when are we going hiking?"

"Soon," he said. Then he smiled. "While Amy is in casts would be a good time."

I laughed. "Right on."

I thought about Amy. And I thought about her father. She had missed out on a lot. "But maybe one day, Dad, you could take her on a hiking trip. You know, just a father and daughter sort of thing?"

He looked surprised. "You wouldn't mind?"

"No," I told him. "Not anymore."

Dayle Campbell Gaetz is the author of many books for children including *Mystery from History, Barkerville Gold, No Problem* and her latest mystery, *Alberta Alibi*. Dayle loves boating and over the years has owned a tiny inflatable raft, a canoe, four sailboats, eleven powerboats and a thirty-two-foot cabin cruiser. Dayle lives in Campbell River, British Columbia.

New
Orca Currents Novel

Wired by Sigmund Brouwer

I cut left to miss a boulder sticking out of the snow. I ducked beneath a branch. I hit a jump at freeway speed. It launched me into the air at least one story off the ground. I leaned forward and made sure my skis stayed straight.

I thumped back to earth and crouched low, so I would block less wind. At this speed, the trees on each side of the slope seemed like flashing fence boards.

Halfway down the run I knew I was skiing the best I ever had. If I kept pushing, I would easily stay at number one.

Beneath my helmet, I grinned my grin of fear. And as I cut into a steep turn, I saw it. But couldn't believe it.

Wire. Black wire stretched between two trees at waist height. I was flashing toward it at thirty meters per second. Hitting the wire at that speed would slice me in two.

New
Orca Currents Novel

Flower Power by Ann Walsh

Why did everyone keep asking me how I felt? How did they expect me to feel? I felt rotten. I felt worried. I felt scared.

Worried about what I was going to feed Mom for lunch and dinner and breakfast the next day and the day after that and the day after that. Worried about who would buy the groceries when we ran out of milk and bread. Worried about how Mom was going to get to the bank, or pay for my swimming lessons, or book my flight to see Dad next month or do anything at all if she wasn't going to come down from that tree.

Scared about her falling and hurting herself.

And very, very scared about what my friends would say when they found out what was going on.

How did I feel? What a dumb question.

New
Orca Currents Novel

Sudden Impact by Lesley Choyce

The heavy fullback went down right on top of him. I heard this terrifying scream come out of Kurt. Kurt was not usually a screamer. I'd never heard him utter the slightest whimper of pain, ever. He was as tough as they come.

A whistle blew. The ball had missed the net. Nobody knew what I knew. I was over the rickety fence and running onto the field. The referee pulled the Fairview goon off of Kurt, but Kurt was still curled over on the grass.

Coach Kenner yelled at me to get off the field. He and Jason both came chasing after me. They thought I'd lost my mind. A kid falls down in a soccer game, big deal. But I knew better.